A dynamic range of nev
emerging writers, this
lights. The themes and p
Rooted in close observa
concern the 'unexplored
must for anyone who likes good writing.

> Nancy Gaffield, author of *Tokaido Road*, winner of the
> 2011 Aldeburgh First Collection Prize

Unexplored Territory

Also by Maria C. McCarthy

strange fruits (2011)
Nothing But (2007)
Learning to be English (2006, 2008)
All Sorts (ed.) (2005)

Unexplored Territory

Poetry and fiction from Cultured Llama

Edited by Maria C. McCarthy

Cultured Llama Publishing

First published in 2012 by
Cultured Llama Publishing
11 London Road
Teynham, Sittingbourne
ME9 9QW
www.culturedllama.co.uk

Collection: Copyright © 2012 Cultured Llama Publishing
Individual contributions: Copyright © 2012 by the individual authors
All rights reserved

The right of the individual authors to be identified as the authors of this work has been asserted by them in accordance with Section 77 of the Copyright, Designs and Patents Act 1988

All characters appearing in this work, other than those in the public domain, are fictitious and any resemblance to real persons, living or dead, is purely coincidental

No reproduction of any part of this book may take place, whether stored in a retrieval system, or transmitted in any form, or by any means, electronic, mechanical, photocopying, recording or otherwise, without prior written permission from Cultured Llama Publishing

A CIP record for this book is available from The British Library

This book is sold subject to the conditions that it shall not, by way of trade or otherwise, be lent, re-sold, hired out, or otherwise circulated without the publisher's prior consent in any form of binding or cover other than that in which it is published and without a similar condition including this condition being imposed on the subsequent purchaser

ISBN 978-0-9568921-7-1

Cover painting by Maggie Drury

Printed in Great Britain by Lightning Source UK Ltd

Contents

Foreword   xi

Poetry

Fiona Sinclair
When a Sex Symbol Takes to Sensible Shoes   3
Singing Group   4

Jenny Cross
A Coach Trip to Beth Chatto's Garden on a Wet Day   5
Fat Woman   6
Perfection   8

Mark Holihan
A Memory for Breakfast   10
The Shining Sea   11
Independence Day   13

Gillian Moyes
Snail Shell on the Pilgrims' Way   14
Mary Anning   15

Richard Thomas
Flamingo   16
Twenty Five   18
Arise to thy Lyre   19

Jane Stemp
Judgement   20
Festival at Presteigne   21

Luigi Marchini
  Search   22
    I Where is my Nymph?   22
    II Bed Sit   23
    III Gillingham   25
    IV End Game   26
  History Recalls How Cruel the Flood Can Be   27

Hilda Sheehan
  The House that Died   28
  The Seal   29

Sarah Jenkin
  Medway Mermaid   30

Philip Kane
  River's Edge   31
  From city's little heart   32
    johnnie & carole have a row   32
    carole in the supermarket   32
    being johnnie means   33
    a note from carole to the author   33

Maria C. McCarthy
  Pioneer   35
  There are Boats on the Orchard   36

Rosemary McLeish
  Charcoal Drawing   38

June English
  Sabbath   40
  Higher Nature   42

Bethany W. Pope
   Hollows   43
   Radiance   47

Maggie Harris
   The Laughter of Black Women   52
   My Daughters: A Poem for Mother's Day   53

Vicky Wilson
   Karaoke Poetry   55
      I Will Survive   55
      Wish You Were Here   56
      Like a Rolling Stone   57

Fiction

Maggie Harris
   The Calypsonians of Ramsgate   61

Maggie Drury
   Unexplored Territory   68

Maria C. McCarthy
   Cold Salt Water   77

Jane Stemp
   Aftermath   81

Biographies of the Authors   89

Acknowledgements   93

Foreword

Unexplored Territory is a very personal selection. The poems and stories are those that stood out from book proposals sent to Cultured Llama, as well as invited submissions from authors whose work I admire. Some of these writers recommended others whom I might approach. It emerged as a kind of chain letter of good writing.

There was no theme set for this anthology, yet themes emerged. Water – with its real, mystical and mythical possibilities – pervades Luigi Marchini's 'History recalls how cruel the flood can be', Sarah Jenkin's 'Medway Mermaid' and Hilda Sheehan's 'Seal'. The opening of Jane Stemp's 'Aftermath' takes place near water, too, when two people, damaged by war in different ways, meet on Magdalen Bridge; but Stemp's story is more about displacement, which is the overarching theme of this anthology.

Mark Holihan's 'Independence Day' sees an exiled American thinking: "America and I don't talk any more./ Maybe it's because I live in England and Uncle Sam never calls". An Irish mother whose son is beaten on the night of the Guildford pub bombings in my story, 'Cold Salt Water', finds her boy is now "approved to British standards", like the condoms she finds in his drawer. Maggie Drury's 'Unexplored Territory' is packed with outsiders who spy on their neighbours, depict them in paintings, fantasise about them, yet fail to engage in normal relationships.

Thanks are due to Anne-Marie Jordan for casting a copy-editing eye over the anthology, Maggie Drury for the cover image and Bob Carling for cover and book design. Thanks most of all to the authors who have made this such an exciting project; I am delighted to present writing of such diversity and consistent high quality.

As Nancy Gaffield points out, 'this anthology offers numerous delights'. Dip in and enjoy.

Maria C. McCarthy

Poetry

When a Sex Symbol Takes to Sensible Shoes

Suddenly across the store, through a middle aged
bottle glass blur, I spot blonde hair familiar as a logo,
but hesitate unable to make out that fantasy body
drawn by an adolescent boy on his exercise book.
Close up, these photographs from *The Misfits*
are like meeting an old friend after a debilitating illness.
Trademark eyeliner has become heavy, shutters closing
on the empty windows of a house whose occupant has left.
Her body still forms a perfect 8 but is not gift wrapped
in gold lamé, instead she is a hillbilly's wife in white cotton
Sunday dress posing in a Steinbeck farmyard.
Looking down the barrel of the camera,
lips no longer part in the throes of an orgasmic O,
but are forced into a localised smile.
The confection of a single 1950s' picture
draws my eyes like wasps to a baker's window,
leaving me craving other heyday poses, addictive as sugar.
Paying my last respects to the snapshots from her final film,
I notice, more shocking than being shared around
like a joint by the Kennedy boys' club, her comfortable shoes.

Fiona Sinclair

Singing Group

Given the note by our own Gareth Malone,
we slide up and down the scales
like nervous skaters.
Once again death
has positively discriminated against woman
so that twelve men
must do the heavy lifting in *Old Man River*.
At break, called up for tea duty,
an ex-teacher duo
red faced and glazed eyed
deal with temperamental urn and
requests for coffee.
In loose groups, couples on mouth watering
pensions share cruise ship stories
whilst Pearl and Pamela dote on grandchildren.
Showered with *Good Byes* and *Have a good week,*
it is as if I've spent the afternoon
in an Ealing film.
Homeward, I pass a young couple
in wax jackets walking Labradors,
my *Hello* ignored as they pass me.

Fiona Sinclair

A Coach Trip to Beth Chatto's Garden on a Wet Day

Spears of rain dance on motorway grey.
Denim blue clouds rest on billowing trees.
Inside the bus, the twitter and hum of comfy voices
like the sound of the sea, like a lullaby.
And the powdered widows, brave and bright
sit among the marrieds, gazing separately out.

They have nice tight perms,
and pull ingenious hair over slack skin,
clutch the *Daily Telegraph,* pak-a-mac and flask of tea.
Latin is the grammar of this group,
'Dictamnus albus.'
'I had it but it didn't do.'
'Parahebe perfoliata.'
'Wonderful plant!'
'This my first time.'
'What's the café like?'
'I don't care as long as I can buy plants.'

Then drift away, leave them to the guided tour.
Lose myself in crowds of roses, gangs of ferns,
hordes of clamouring grasses,
delphiniums, geraniums.
Under a flickering canopy of leaves,
the rain lances fiercely into the lake.

Jenny Cross

Fat Woman

I wish I could be fat
and feel soft folds of flesh
embrace my bones.
The warm billows of my breasts
would comfort me as I moved about.
My juicy plump buttocks, a cushion when I sat.

Soft folds of chins, quivering,
when I laughed they'd ripple like a shaken jelly.
I wish I could be fat.
To roll majestically down the street
barging into rude boys who stare.
With one flip of my hip
I'd send them running for cover.
I wish I could be fat!

Small children could lie in my vast lap,
hide under the pillows of my arms,
climb the pillars of my sturdy legs.
My sausage hands will knead
great mounds of dough, I will
rise, like bread.
And be fat.

Not just yet – crispbread (no bread)
semi everything, half not whole.
Reduced.
Skimmed.
Low.

Virtually.
Free.

But, I wish I could be fat.
I *could* be fat.

Jenny Cross

Perfection

He brought her sea glass,
packets of tea.
A bag of cherries, a stone
with a hole, threaded on
blue twine.

He grew sweetcorn, beetroot,
rosy lettuce,
pink poppies like
crumpled underwear,
and small, sweet peas.

He poured her wine,
buttered biscuits,
fed her grapes,
cheese soufflé.
And chocolate mousse.

He held her when she cried, called
when he was late.
And for her birthday,
a surprise picnic.
With pink balloons.

But.

He always left the seat up,
towels on the floor,
marmalade on the plate,
crumbs in the butter.
Finished her sentences.
But
that was when she loved him best.

Jenny Cross

A Memory for Breakfast

A sideways look,
your grin is compressed,
the heat of your arm as it's pressed
to mine burns deliciously
into my flesh.
Like midday sun in Kinshasa
where sane dogs and we,
non-English, lunched comfortably
in air-conditioned dining rooms,
'Come sit here, next to me.'

This morning you turn to laugh,
sun catching your smile
and your fingers angled on the lip of a cup,
black tea steaming like Congo earth
after the rain
where you danced in glittering sandals
between clinking tables
with warbling Soukous music throbbing
and all the shiny eyes watching
the sequins on your sari flashing
beaded silk swinging from your hips
moving like the music
and red as lust.
'Hey Mama yangu, stay dance with me.'

Mark Holihan

The Shining Sea

Two days ago I flew back
from your quiet marina
through Andalucian rain.
As the jet rose, cold sun climbed
above the terracotta horizon,
sharp as a broken tile
or a conversation stopped
by the closing glass doors
in Malaga's polished airport.

Now this winter-crusted car
passes islands in the traffic.
Crocuses push through the grass,
tiny paper crowns re-grown
from the litter of parties neither of us recall.
I drive past iridescent crows
who stalk the morning sun across
translucent leaves on roundabouts.
The hard light bounces off windows
and shatters across windscreens
and even the sea, heaving and muttering
in its bright, spangled distance.

The sea still ties us,
wearing away at bridges and time
as you sit on it feeling the waves
lapping against Maria Teresa's hull
with the sound of your children's heartbeats.
The seventh wave is the biggest,
one for each of your children.
As children ourselves we counted them
on wide, white beaches to catch the longest ride,
and sometimes the biggest fall.

And still we say it is as though
no time has passed even if
I've long lost count of the waves
from where I sit in my house watching.
But you don't watch,
you ride them still, saying
'You can never go back'
even if we both know
we have never left.

Mark Holihan

Independence Day

So I'm driving in Pfizer traffic
down the A256 with
Willie Nelson on the radio singing
'Good morning America how are you...'
and when I join in there are tears in my eyes
'Don't you know me, I'm your native son...'

I don't know, America and I don't talk any more.
Maybe it's because I live in England, but Uncle Sam never calls,
nor Uncle Bob, or Cousin Jimmy
and poor Aunt Mary died almost two years ago now
just before brother Bill divorced for the third time
and his ex-wife, Dr Liz, took off to Oregon with the family silver
and my dead Mom's cat, Sambo.

Still Willie and I are singing.
I think he's off key.
And it's no wonder Uncle Sam and I don't talk, really.
How could we hear each other over the rumble
of tanks and the singing of hymns?
Maybe this native son is confused.
So, I'm driving between dripping hedgerows
and wailing with Willie while ignoring the passing stares
because Uncle Bob made the best cheeseburgers
and there are sailboats on San Francisco Bay
and the fog drips off the redwoods
in the Santa Cruz mountains
in a tiny patter
of profound silence.

Mark Holihan

Snail Shell on the Pilgrims' Way

Like white bone china,
an empty dish
discarded by the thrush

ending a snail's slow pilgrimage
from leaf to leaf,
its brown patterns of whorls
pecked clean by wind and rain.

It calls to mind the journeys
of other lives, who left no trace
of a silvery trail nor a shell –
this relic tucked in my pocket,

but then I discover the monk
resting on a bench in the sun,
his paunchy body and rope-tied cassock
sculpted from remains of an oak.

I lean against him –
it's a wonderment, Brother,
that we've grown and flown,
crawled and walked here at all.

Gillian Moyes

Mary Anning

1799 – 1847

Superstition said a strike of lightning
brightened your eyes, led you to find us.
Child of the shoreline, drenching the hem
of patched petticoats, you exhumed us from cliffs,
called us snake-stones and verteberries,
knew in your bones our true value
when you scrubbed us, swapped us for pennies
as curios for Lyme Regis tourists.

Of course men of letters seized the limelight,
gave us names such as ichthyosaurus
you couldn't pronounce let alone spell.
Survivor of landslides, incoming tides,
girl with ragged fingernails,
you dug us out of darkness.

Gillian Moyes

Flamingo

Flesh-coloured shrimp eater,
wide-winged wired bird,
raking the dirt pedalling the earth,
knee-knobbled beanpole legs,
knee being ankle joint,
long wavy bright length,
herds of necks pushed right back,
heads out, all in one leg,
vibrancy curved pink spinner,
beak in the ground like a compass,
dot-eyed wading follower,
feather-liced idoliser,
tall social armpit sleeper,
delightful eyeful not quite parrot,
ancient Roman delicacy,
great poignant egg defender,
living embodiment of Ra,
popular plastic lawn ornament,
iconic worshipped filter-feeder,
underwater insect sucker,
upside down water drainer,
thirty seven miles per hour flapper,
Africa North America
Central America Europe
South America Asia,
lava-loving ice bird,
mud mounder by mouthful,
cunningly undesirable,
thirty years of male looking female,

thirty years of female looking male,
many accidental bisexual nights,
lethargy-enthused strawberry sunset
pinking the waters forever.

Richard Thomas

Twenty Five

Prelude to a Sunday morning

I am in tropical rooms
amongst the sickly spices
that clog my fleeting air.
In the fruit shade windows

amongst the sickly spices,
the black cat of English night.
In the fruit shade, windows
moon-eyed. With starline smile

the black cat of English night
hums a calypso. I retreat,
moon-eyed with starline smile.
My love with rose in her hair

hums a calypso. I retreat,
blossoming into the night like
my love with rose in her hair:
a rich red drop in oaky water.

Richard Thomas

Arise to thy Lyre

On visiting The Protestant Cemetery, Rome

Souls steam
from the soil
like Heaven's own perfume;
only the poets can make death
smell sweet.

I want
to throw my eyes
upon the graves of them
and seize an illumination
of words.

I sit
beneath an air
rich with archaic shades
thinking of the romantics who
ate beef.

Richard Thomas

Judgement

after Rubens

Make, in this threefold grace,
not one decision but two.

Look wisdom in the face
and say, not you, not you.

The apple spun in the hand
the heel turned in the dust,

beauty, the harshest command,
makes choice fall where it must.

Time stretches cold and slow
pushes the air like glass

bending the light like a bow
making the future pass.

Wisdom and faith both deny
what the back of the brain has to do

but the world and the apple roll by,
waiting for you, for you.

Jane Stemp

Festival at Presteigne

for Cecilia McDowall on her sixtieth birthday

After the flood,
in still water
one single drop
rings trees with time,

hollowing the past until
water-haunted, bell-rung
in caves of echo
stones sound, resound, and circles
widen. An hour

of minutes, a now of years:
leaves rustle like cards,
the nine of memory
slips from the pack, hunting
notes that fly like birds

under a slanting sky.
Through hills strung with cloud
the buzzard and the dove
descend.

Jane Stemp

Search

I Where is my Nymph?

I trudge through fields
green brown with grass, mud, shit:
the garden of England. As I

slog on
I breathe in
gulping gasps;
my legs start to waver.
I sit on a pyre
of leaves, take off my boots
look up at the full-bellied clouds,
newly formed,
as they rotate slowly
then fast, faster
until a bright light oscillates at their centres.
I want to jump up into them.
All around me silhouettes
of lions, eagles, llamas, penguins
gravitate towards the sky.

'Why not me?'

At Greenwich now
and on the great river
I see the domes of the Old Royal Naval College,
miniature St Paul's;
for the first time since I left
the sun cleaves through the moving cloud-rack
polishing the city.
Should I search the boxes at Waterloo,
sort through the rubbish, the needles
or inhale asbestos

in Battersea's Power Station?
Its four chimneys like rockets ready for take off,
a long countdown. I imagine
the entrance's marble floor
no longer swept by cleaners,
the mess hall full of 1983 *Daily Mails*,
dirty cups, abandoned helmets,
all time warped.
Or should I plunge into the Thames,
swim past the mudlarks,
the cormorants' nests
under London Bridge,
and through the silt

of your history,
to find her?

I notice
how striking the junction
of building and cloud is.

II Bed Sit

The room seems to welcome
his presence, hesitantly,
like the specious smile of a sales rep;
sun gleaming through the skylight,
light thrown back from the settee
and the armchair's ragged upholstery;
thrown back by the foot wide mirror on
the far wall, between Constable's *Haywain*
and some picture that looks
like a giant upside-down snail.
Tracing her here took months.
Still he isn't sure.

He scans the room for signs.
Losing her was easier
than this infinite search for remnants.
He breathes the breath of the room;
stale tobacco,
rotten woodwork
odour of damp lino and mildew,
the musty smell of underground vaults.

Slowly, ciphers reveal
themselves, presents
from a procession
of guests
       long gone:
on the wall, small fingerprints;
a splattered stain
raying like the shadow of a bursting bomb.
On the mirror the name 'Jade' scratched
in the bottom right corner, with God knows what.
Cigarette burns on the pine table. He walks

to the wash basin,
opens the small cabinet above,
emptying it of ten hairpins or so,
redundant things,

to the wardrobe – nothing.
Then the bedside cabinet,
finding two boiled sweets,
and under the bed –
a soiled football programme
stuffed under one of the legs.

Sitting on the bare mattress
he looks around one last time
and catches a scent,

something different,
familiar,
a cheap perfume
he had bought for her?

He stretches out his arms.
The scent does not linger
long enough for him to savour it.

III Gillingham

The train left London's
greyness
passing buildings, gloomy,
dormant, sun now trapped in their
confines like a caged peacock.
I hadn't expected more of the same.
As it crossed the river
and passed through
Clapham, Brixton, Wandsworth,
bedraggled tenements, graffiti, waste.
I had visions
of a nomadic bird finally settling,
then the train stopped here.

I stare out of the window as if I could
see you but I don't even know your
address, just that you live
here.
And you –
as colourful as a Chagall window
and as soft as an insect's wings –
can you see me?

IV End Game

Now
he doesn't look for her anymore,
has stopped staring at the imprints of her feet
on the bedroom carpet,
cannot hear her voice, her laughter,
in the crackle of the leaves in the garden,
or in the scuttling of the mice in the shed.

Now
he cannot see her,
photos thrown away along with
the inscribed copy of Neruda's *Captain's Verses*,
Joni Mitchell's *Blue* (a gift from her)
and the red blouse he bought her one Christmas.
Had she ever worn it?

At times he thinks he catches
her scent on the bed sheets,
feels her fingers on his back,
tastes her lipstick;
when this happens he gets up.
switches on the light
makes the bed.

Luigi Marchini

History Recalls How Cruel the Flood Can Be

We built a house out of
wet books, sodden
after the creek
burst its banks.

The water took,
still loots,
everything
except these books which
we can no longer read.
The balls of cloud

blackened, bleak (were they ever bright?)
carry on bleeding lumps
of despair from which
there is
no shelter. Still.

There is a hole in the roof
but no rainbow to marvel at;
the wheelbarrow
floats away along with
the second edition *Moby-Dick*

while a large boat sails past.

Luigi Marchini

The House that Died

One day, our house stopped breathing.
A passer-by noticed it going blue
as noise escaped from an open window:
a gasp, a choke.

People came out –
patted it on the back, made suggestions:

'Cut the hedge down, tidy the garden,
weed it, scrape it, paint it a brilliant white –
don't walk on the grass for God's sake!'

'Punch it in the chest, electrocute it, stick
a knife in its throat – insert a straw, then blow.'

Nothing helped.
The council pronounced it dead
in its corner plot. *It just gave up the will to be a home.*

How it suffered – tried so hard to breathe,
make space, be tidy, stylish, organised –
look nice like other houses on the street.

It went stiff and black quite quickly;
flesh fell from its frame,
like bricks toppling from a tall building.

In the silence of our grief, we chased flies off its back,
left the bones for a viewing, no funeral though.

Hilda Sheehan

The Seal

Sometimes,
the seal from next door borrows my bathtub
to loll in cool water. He says, 'there's nowhere left
to get wet' and lets himself in with the key I leave
in a dried up sea under broken corrugated coral.

When I get home,
I close the mouth of the loo; sit and watch
him swish this way and that; his fat, wet behind
rises up and down like a barren island in a storm,
sending waves to me –

the kind that make you want to club the wicked,

or throw a fish.

Later,
when only his head can be seen,
we talk in ripples that circle him;
silence our lost worlds.

I don't know why he comes, it's not as if we're lovers:
he's a seal, and I just live here.

Hilda Sheehan

Medway Mermaid

You've probably heard about my flowing
hair. And my silvery scales. But
has anyone ever told you about my
teeth, my darling?
My mother was mated with a great
white. She says: *He tracked me out on the coral
reef.* My lips trace the gash in her
belly: *ask no questions. It brought me
you,* she says. She says: *you chewed your
way out.* That's why I'm here on this rock, neither
fish nor fowl.
I can look after myself, darling. I don't
need you to protect me;
when mermaids smile, we
bare our teeth.

Sarah Jenkin

River's Edge

The boat is half-sunk, tipped into the river
like a pail to gather water. At low
tide, soft waves still lap to halfway up the
rowing bench. Mud sucks hungrily at the
rest. This vessel, shattered at the edge where
two worlds slowly fence, echoes like a soul's
small voice against the river's breast. The smell
of the mud, cabbage-rot, merges with the
crack of nearby sails. Into the space flows
an air of melancholy, loss, fallen
generations gone into the mud and
tide of history. Their long shadow flicks
through the shallows like an eel; a substance
that eludes the moment's grasp to haunt me.

Philip Kane

From 'city's little heart'

johnnie & carole have a row

johnnie losing too much money
at cards carole throwing his
guitar from the window of
their second floor flat johnnie
hitting her and saying she's
a stupid bitch carole sleeping
with another man because she's
angry carole shouting i love
you i love you as
johnnie slams the door behind
him and stamps down the
stairs to the street johnnie
getting pissed and breaking windows
johnnie going home because there's
nowhere else and it's raining

carole in the supermarket

carole is pushing a trolley
johnnie wouldn't come with her
so she pretends she's forgotten
about buying booze
queues up behind the old ladies
who clutch boxes of bakewell tarts
as if it's the only vice they have left
the girl at the checkout
is called mandy and wears
a thick gold ring on every finger
when she picks each item up
to check the price
she crushes it between her rings
as if it is the supermarket
and she is giant with hate

being johnnie means

wearing a leather jacket
even on the hottest days
sometimes carrying a crash helmet
but not owning a motorbike
reading the novels of
kathy acker and jack kerouac
playing the guitar
busking in brighton
being seen at the right gigs
talking about drugs
as if you've tried them all
at least once
walking with a swagger
being moody
and never dancing

a note from carole to the author

personally i believe
you are too cynical by far
and that makes your picture
of me wholly inaccurate

also you misunderstand johnnie
at least he believes
in himself and hates tories
he isn't bad just looking

for something and maybe
he's mostly bemused
like everyone in this town
by the way i'm a writer too

why can't you include
one of my love poems
it would brighten up
this sequence and

give me a break
please think of our feelings
regards
carole

Philip Kane

Pioneer

There was snow this time last year.
I watched as a woodpecker knocked

ten bells out of a dead tree in the orchard,
stark green and red in a virgin world.

Blue tits and blackbirds feasted on fat balls
suspended in cages from the car port.

The woodpecker remained beyond the post
and wire frontier where the orchard ends

and the garden begins. Now, in the bare earth
beneath the rotary clothes line, perfect circles,

formed by the diamond drill of a border-
crossing pioneer, staking a claim, or foraging

old territory, unwilling to relinquish lost land.

Maria C. McCarthy

There are Boats on the Orchard

(i)
Tarpaulin stretched over hull, on twin wheels
with one flat tyre, tilted starboard,
a parched prow points towards the water
butt that catches the run-off from the outhouse roof.

It's seen the turning of the seasons twice
in this spot across from its mate that nestles
in the hedgerow, mast scraping hawthorn.

(ii)
The farmer's in the orchard with a man
and van with *Drainage Solutions* inscribed
on the side. A handshake, then *Solutions*
man hooks hedgerow boat to trailer,
tacks between the blossoming trees.

(iii)
There was a speedboat, too, that should have been
cresting the waves at Whitstable, but sat so long
in the gap by the broken-down horse box
that I noticed neither its presence, nor absence,
till a policeman neighbour saw paperwork
at the station, relating to its liberation.

(iv)
There were floods in fifty-three.
Hundreds of sheep were drowned
due to loss of local knowledge,
left to graze on marshland

reclaimed by the estuary
that lies between the mainland
where the orchard stands
and the Isle of Sheppey.

(v)
One grass-locked vessel
waits for the waters to swell.

Maria C. McCarthy

Charcoal Drawing

He huddles in the hospital bed,
his breath hardly ruffling the sheets,
tubes sneaking and snaking into and
out of orifices and veins, pale as
the cadaver he will shortly become.
His voice, reduced today to a faded
whisper, beckons me forward, pleads:
what about that ticket to Switzerland?

Every visit he asks if I've brought it;
and every visit he asks for the last
charcoal drawing he drew with his
daughter, even in his blindness,
so advanced now he has to grope
for his three o'clock cup of tea.

Ah, now, he says, look at the trees,
see the shimmering light, the path
through the woods, the people.
I look at his usual Pissarro-like landscape,
the branches soaring out of the
buzzing, blooming confusion of leaves,
the rubbed-out sun smudging the lane
with light and shade, the faintest
hint of a couple walking into the woods.

It's lovely, I say, one of your best.
We both did it, he answers, me and
Frances together. He turns the drawing
this way and that, asks me: Is this
the side with the dog? I'm not sure
I see a dog, but he says, That's hers,
and the other side's mine.

In these last days he has only one regret:
that he made his pictures too dark.
Never mind, I say, wait till you get
your cataracts done, your paintings
will dazzle us with their blaze and
brilliance, your daffodils fizz with light.
No, he shakes his head, humouring me,
I'll be in Switzerland before then.

As a girl, I tell him, I went to Switzerland.
In the heat of a summer afternoon, we rode
a cable car above Grünewald, where
the flowers in the alpine meadows
spread under our feet like tapestries,
like dreams. The joy of his boyhood was
berry-picking in Perthshire: the music
the rain played on the tin roofs of the bothies,
the tales told companionably in the night,
the sun in the morning rainbowing the drops
on each blade of grass, each flower.
All this appeared in drawing after drawing,
painting after painting, as he tried to
lay his brief vision of Eden before us.

I hold his hand. No more fairy tales. Yes,
I agree, you'll be in Switzerland before then.

Rosemary McLeish

Sabbath

I've come to terms with living death,
learned to play the M.S. game,
the two steps forward, ten steps back.
What I need now's a benison –
if you can truly walk on water,
feed five thousand with two fishes,
lend my hands the strength to paint –

the odds aren't great. I've little hope,
but if you *did* raise Lazarus,
heal the Centurion's man by proxy –
for all my sakes, let the Botox work –
let science have its miracles,
do it so my blindness sees.

I'm sick to death of vassalage,
my palette waits, I need your help
to recreate myself through colour,
in gold and red and aubergine,
ripe blackberries and stubble-fields.

I'll travel where my brushstrokes take me –
portray the Magdalene in crimson silk,
meet John the Baptist, arms outstretched
to rebirth me in Jordan's waters –

I'll portray the Red Sea's buoyant flow –
draw the leper you made whole,
paint a path towards my Maker.

We'll sit at God's right hand and share
the marriage wine you changed from water –

and on the Sabbath day I'll rest.

June English

Higher Nature

Behind the Post-Office, that's where she lives,
a handsome woman with a wooden leg,
russet hair as deep as leaves in autumn.
Her ruling passion's cosmic consciousness,
organic wholeness, bonding with the universe,
or so the doctor says and he should know:
his car is often seen outside the house.

But not a word about the wooden leg:
except to say he finds it most intriguing.
He's been acting rather strange these last few weeks,
stands for hours, embracing nature, arms outstretched,
rumour has it he sometimes does it naked.
The leg? Oh yes, the handsome woman claims
it's a miracle, a triumph of Higher Nature,
grafted on when she was still a child.
Her blood has mingled with the apple's sap:
she sheds her skin in winter to be reborn in spring.

I make her clothes: she wears those see-through things,
with suns and moons and planets where it counts -
and by the way, the limb is quite fantastic,
hand-carved from da Vinci's *Larynx and Leg*.
Don't quote me, but the doctor's wife is worried,
he's started burning incense, chanting *om... m...*
says that he seeks organic ecstasy.
And from the look of things I'd say he's found it.

June English

Hollows

I distracted myself, walking
into the wind, by remembering
a story my grandfather told me
about the ancestor brothers
who came over from England
to give us our name.

They were loners,
all three of them,
and though Charleston
was, at that time,
the only real town,
there was too much
Society for one brother.

John Pope split off
from the others,
packed gun and ruck sack,
a good skinning knife,
and headed out West.

He landed in the mountainous
territory that would eventually
be named Kentucky
and though there was Society
there already waiting for him,
it was more to his taste,

speaking a language
that sprang up from the land.
He refused their help
to build a longhouse,
choosing instead a giant oak.

The trunk was fifteen feet
in diameter; he hollowed it out.
Fire, like death,
was ever our friend.

He lived there for twenty years
before his native bride
finally convinced him
to take up
a more human residence.

There were more
whites there now,
and although they
shunned him, he had
become a racial mediator,

his bilingual children
needed their status.
That is how the world
gets us all, in the end.
It burns up our heartwood.

Musing on this
carried me miles,
across the bleak
Virginia highway
the snow had
made waste.

I imagined that I still
felt my fingers.
Head down in flurries,
I trundled on.

My torn sneakers
swathed over in duct tape,
my jeans wet to the thigh
where my feverish heat
melted the snow.

My toes were a dream
I had once,
my hands balled
in the joined front pocket
of my five-dollar hoodie.

My university was closed
for a week and I had
nowhere to go,
no money to take me.

My backpack was weighed down
with poetry, novels, what food
I could scrounge, a blanket,
matches, my grandfather's
bone-handled knife.

There was an unused
cemetery near by
that I thought likely.
The newest grave
was a hundred years old.

It belonged to a child,
a lamb carved
in sandstone,
a few close dates.

I climbed over
the tottering fence
and landed in powder
that flew up in a spray

that was joyous,
rainbowed in moonlight.
I turned from the road
and found my tree.

It was a yew,
evergreen, decorated
with a few withered berries
that faced me like eyes,
inviting me in.

There was a crack,
a fox-den, waiting for me,
empty. I cleared
out the bracken,
lit my small fire

which held me
the week, heating my soup
and lighting my poetry
as I lay, curled and warm,
in that beating heart,
at home with the dead.

Bethany W. Pope

Radiance

I have seen photographs
describing a fragment
of the way they were then,
my uncle and father,
Danny and John.
The doctor of not-yet,
the future minister,
dressed country presentable,
more fifties than sixties,
with scrimped hair cut high and tight,
spiked by their grandfather
who couldn't stand a handbreadth of locks
on the head of a boy.
It was their first year in Florida

inhabiting a home I came to know well,
when I lived there, half grey-blue wood,
half brick and painted cinderblock;
that wide, sprawling yard of hibiscus,
myrtle, orange trees – still replete
with elephant ear that Popie had not vanquished –
ferns, the square rose garden in the corner
their father never gave up on,
to spite the environment, that light sandy soil
so different from mountains
where if the land was sweet, where
you'd drop a flower and a shrub would flourish,
fed by unseen source.

The boys were curious, a little too daring.
I have no idea where they found
the magazine which sold Army Surplus.
I've no idea where they came up with the cash,
but somehow or other they scrimped it together,

along with stamped envelope, an address card
messily filled in by dyslexic hands.

I could not have stood the waiting they endured,
all those weeks of processing. Their little card
filtering through the guts
of some vast company,
denuded of its sweat-stained,
green florals. Knowing my father's
life-long impatience he probably hounded
the postman to ruinous depression,
wondering out loud, when the poor man
showed his overheated adult face,
if the package had been missed.

Eventually it came round,
as all things do,
wrapped in brown paper,
addressed by hand.
Danny was older, his privilege to open,
sliding his knife blade scalpel-like through twine,
revealing a small round can,
the kind home-movie film came in,
sealed off tight.

John was the one to uncover the sacrament,
and what shone there alone in the bottom,
naturally inspired
religious awe and adoration.
It lit up his face like a mosaic veil
and made brother Danny
fall back as though stricken.
John sucked in his breath.

A small disc of incredible radiation,
a glowing light that could never be

extinguished or hidden,
that the boys, or anyone,
could never make dwindle
or in any way diminish.
Light without heat, that anyway
burned them,
a host of slow poison to hold on the palm.

They stood alone together,
made isolate by silence,
hands of the same size and substance
clasped, impressed with sharp nails
that could belong to either of them.

They never really played with it.
Popie came in from his job
reclaiming the neglected, placing the broken,
the brain-damaged, deranged
in jobs that they could handle,
according to capacity.
He saw the light, and knew what it was.

He did not yell, or strike them.
He did not even cover it with can-lid.
He knelt down,
hands that struggled at nurturing
settling down on twin curvatures of spine.
He laid out the danger
there on the table, home to toxic feast
and familial rite of pleasure at meals.

When he had finished
describing his horror
my father reached out,
white-cheeked, trembling,
his eyelids glistening,

raw and bright.
He closed the lid tight.

There was already treasure
in that yard.
They added worth
by burying this surfeit.
The boys dug down
deep to plant this seed,
shovels flying
until they hit the water table.

They set it down,
like Hebrew priests
wilfully forgetting
the location of the Ark,
wilfully forgetting that power
such as this
has a way of seeping out.

The light, Springish,
like the sun seen through leaves,
never went out.
It is glowing still, somewhere,
waiting to be found.
Eventually, when I lived there,
I would seek it out.

In the places I looked I found:
a roundel of imported flint,
a similar chunk of rose quartz,
the soggy remains of Popie's first garden,
the spilled ancient slag
of a conquistador foundry,
the skull of a large dog,
a horse tooth,

five ring-neck serpents, still alive,
and the rusted husk
of a Volkswagen side mirror.

I am still looking,
still scouring the depths
for that dangerous light,
which I have never seen,
though I have felt its intimations.
I have faith I shall do,
when the time is right.
In the meantime I will pray
for the recovery of light.[1]

Bethany W. Pope

---

[1] In the early 1960s it was possible to order samples of uranium for a few dollars from Army Surplus catalogues. My father and uncle purchased a specimen, which my grandfather disposed of by burying it in his rose garden, where it presumably seeped into the water table. I spent a good portion of my childhood seeking it out, without success, although I did find other items of interest.

The Laughter of Black Women

The laughter of black women is like nothing else
It is belly source and ocean deep
A tsunami announcing itself
A confluence of rivers

It is dancehall loudhailer
It is Moses parting the waters
It is hurricanes ripping through Cuba
It is the ruins of Babel
Jesus routing the Pharisees
Yemanja claiming the throne

For every nappy-haired child lost in the wilderness
Find such a woman, listen to her laugh

Maggie Harris

My Daughters: A Poem for Mother's Day

My daughters are my beacons
my flagships
my torchbearers;
wearers of my high-heeled shoes
and lipstick
purveyors of my mother's words
warriors for grandmother's bangles
still hanging from my wrist.
In their English eyes shine a South American odyssey
spirits strong as whalebone
souls deep as the Caribbean Sea
voices lyrical as dolphins
flesh no inconsequential lover
can conquer.
My daughters wrestle flat-pack furniture
with the tenacity of Amazons
decode the language of Nanos and iPhones
wrestle baby crocodiles into babygros
eat McDonald's and fry chowmein
with Guyanese cassareep.
They dance limbos with castanets
tread the boards like stars
play pianos and violins to
Bob Marley.
If am stranded on any shore where there is no curry
or mobile phone
I only have to find a high point and howl such a howl
Ginsberg will have nothing on me
and from some midstream current or from some photoshoot

a cry will come and place me firmly
on a rock where Ed Sheeran plays guitar
and grandchildren may or may not notice I am there
but from the sofa a teenage goth
makes sulky room for me,
a small smile at the corner
of her black-lipsticked mouth.

Maggie Harris

Karaoke Poetry

I Will Survive

At first you are afraid, you are petrified.
So I make a notice for your bedsit door –
Jean-Paul Sartre: 'Il est interdit d'avoir peur.'
Bad advice for a boy coming out in 1980s Jamaica, but for now
we're foreign students, holed up in a small French town
where I fill your dreams with my music, Joni and Leonard Cohen,
alabaster aliens, and you don't know how to start to explain
the differences we touch on at night.

Two years later. Kingston. I scratch the surface, see past
some of what I didn't know. The servant's room in a villa garden,
the university pool I gatecrash, let in by the colour of my skin,
ackee and saltfish, gay discos, 'Why you white girls dance so fast?'

As long as you know how to love I know you'll stay alive.
You do not. But me, I still survive.

Gloria Gaynor, I Will Survive *(Perrin and Fakaris), 1978*

Vicky Wilson

Wish You Were Here

Two guys with guitar. Moussaka and chips. Red wine.
Green eyes picks out four notes, repeats four times.
A breath, then we're pounding the drumroll on the table.
Shine on you crazy diamond.

Green eyes picks out four notes, repeats four times.
It's his only English chat-up line:
Shine on you crazy diamond.
And his friend's not bad either.

It's his only English chat-up line.
Yugoslav, picking fruit, send home the cash.
And his friend's not bad either.
Heads the hotel room, tails the beach.

Yugoslav, picking fruit, send home the cash.
I mime the sax, you start to sing.
Heads the hotel room, tails the beach.
Must go for a piss, the tab's on us.

I mime the sax, you start to sing.
Two more nights, they wave us to the bus.
Must go for a piss, the tab's on us.
Victoria Station, 9am – and what are all these people doing?

Late-night chemist, morning-after pill.
A breath, then we're pounding the drumroll on the table.
Remember when you were young, you shone like the sun.
Two guys with guitar. Moussaka and chips. Red wine.

Pink Floyd, Shine On You Crazy Diamond *(Waters, Wright and Gilmour), from the album* Wish You Were Here, *1975*

Vicky Wilson

Like a Rolling Stone

How does it feel to be on your own?
The question floats above my right shoulder, midnight on Willesden High Road
and I'm hurrying home, hoping to shake off this complete unknown,

past the restaurant where I queue for take-away masala dosas,
past the deli where chatting women load up with baklava and okra,
How does it feel, how does it feel, to be on your own?

Footsteps slap the pavement behind me, voice is Irish but I know the line, glance, nod,
Dylan?, then suddenly he's hunched in front of my gas fire,
holed socks planted on the patterned carpet, a mystery, a complete unknown,

smoking my cigarettes, drinking my wine, telling me how his family
couldn't fit round the dinner table, laughter, talk and more talk... and me?
How does it feel to be on your own

night after night watching the mice play on the record deck,
smoking your cigarettes, drinking your wine, stuck
in this room you now call home, a street where you're a complete unknown?

And me... I'm silenced by fear of the contagion of isolation,
of making the wrong moves, of not making it in this cold town,
of giving up and crawling home, of staying forever a complete unknown,
of never escaping how it feels, how it feels, to be on your own.

Bob Dylan, Like a Rolling Stone, *1965*

Vicky Wilson

Fiction

The Calypsonians of Ramsgate

Right, we're in the seventies, and there were these three guys. Three roaring rollicking, arrogant boys with manes of black Irish hair and hands as inconsistent as birds. Eyes rolled at the mention of their names. Teachers expelled them from school. Girls gladly raised their skirts in the back of borrowed Fiestas or behind the waltzers on the ramshackle seafront at night.

These were glory days, when dole cheques went straight in the Red Lion or the Royal Standard, when the promise of a painting and decorating job was mildly appealing, especially in the summer when bare chests on the tops of scaffolding was reality bill-boarding. The freedom of the town was theirs.

Jamie, Drake and Errol; their mother had had a penchant for Hollywood movies and stars, and had pinned her daydreams on her boys even as they continually failed to exhibit any of the romance. But there were plenty of derring-dos, and face it, was Mr Flynn a gentleman?

Seaside towns then were only just beginning to die. Some described them as fading, a sign of the times; who wanted waltzers and creaking Ferris wheels when foreign holidays beckoned? The Costas were cheap, as was Greece, and if you wanted black sand, Lanzarote. So the word on the street about poor old Ramsgate was that it was a *dive*, it was *ranking*. Who the fuck wanted to stay in a place where only the Channel prevented the frogs from finishing what they always wanted to do since fucking Henry's days man? But even as everyone dissed the place, apart from one or two who emigrated to Amsterdam or Wales, none of them would live anywhere else. If you wanted a slice of the good life there was Canterbury and London, there and back in a day. On the train of course, less you knew someone with a motor.

The words that fell off the boys' lips sloshed like the Guinness on the sodden bar towels. Their elbows grew white with ownership on the laminated rosewood, and their leather jackets settled securely on the bar stools they barely perched on, shifting only for the bravest or cutest bit of *stuff* – eyes lined with liquid liner, mouth pale with lip-gloss, hair like Farrah Fawcett's.

The old men raised their rheumy eyes through a haze of cigarette smoke from their dark corners by the door, obliged by the pint Jamie might buy them having just been paid for doing up that flat up Westcliff Road some London punter had bought. The old guys were a fountain of knowledge from Henry Tudor to Hitler, *been there mate, 1944*. And foreign invasions continued to happen each summer; flocks of Scandinavian blondes descending through the channels of the local language school, their tentative steps through the doors of The Standard bringing the conversation to a halt. The glint of Ramsgate sand on those golden arms sent hands reaching deep in pockets for a pound note for a half of shandy. Foreign chicks were the business, they all agreed; here for a few weeks then bingo, gone. Not like those local birds scrounging pints and fags off you all night then glued to your arm when they found out you had a lift to the Bali Hai in Margate. The next thing you know they thought you were fucking going out together! Enough of that shit. Those foreign blokes though, they were a right laugh; see their tight asses in white trousers racing off along the seafront on a Saturday night when your money ran out and you were looking for a laugh.

Friday nights were the business: pound notes fluttered between fingers, packets of Embassy and John Players passed over the bar. Shoulders relaxed and laughter cut across the jukebox playing Hendrix or Springsteen or that Commodores shit the chicks all loved.

But it didn't take much for the place to explode. Some *oik* spilling drink on a jacket, some wanker pushing in. Before you knew it fists were out there, knuckles curled round collars. Depending on how many pints had been consumed, that might be all. But if the mood spread, before you could say Red Rum any chairs or tables that weren't screwed down would be flying like missiles. The times windows were smashed were countless. On a Saturday morning the windows would be boarded up and you'd wander in to face a sullen landlord snapping *no way them bastards coming back in 'ere, fucking banned the lot of 'em*. But you'd catch sight of Jamie swigging a pint at The Royal and catch his eye and say *good last night then?* And he'd grin and say *Bloody right! Arseholes need teaching a lesson*. The ban might last a week or two, but business was business and after a mouthful of warnings the boys would be back there again, leaning their elbows on the bar.

Friday night was disco night; Margate loomed, the Bali Hai, the Gavroche, the Hippocampo. *Anyone going to*

Margate? Taxis were fascist, like Thatcher. Much more appropriate to scrounge a lift from the only one of two blokes who owned a motor. The dance floor was the chance the girls got to catch a guy, fuelled with lagers or Dubonnets, bodies clad in maxi-dresses or low-slung hipster trousers with halter-neck tops. That was the time too to see the divide between the girls who danced round their handbags and those who sat in the dark corners of the disco, heads low with the guys over packets of Rizla and lighters warming minuscule nuggets of hope.

And that's the path the boys went down. Not for them the fascist path of colleges and wanker bankers. This was the one life, see? Who wanted shit like houses and neat drives and two weeks in the Costas? People with jobs and cars were wankers. Life was your mates and beating the state at their game. Their voices, full of resolution, grievances and piss-takes, were left over from the revolution of cheese-cloth shirts, the workers' revolution of Ramsgate. Mick Jagger was a ponce. Ask them round and they took the world to pieces, quoting Nostradamus (who they'd all read, though their former teachers at Holy Cross might have disbelieved this). They were like that Alf Garnett character off the telly. They threw aside fashion and *House Beautiful* magazines with scorn as they forked Vesta curries off their mates' girlfriends with relish.

The girls who loved them fought the good fight. They fell for their energetic beauty, their vociferousness, their disdain, the ripple and conviction of their arguments. They saw the good souls beneath their armadillo skin. Drake's girlfriend Caris in particular, risen to the right of that title by giving birth to little Drake, took his cavalier pretences with good grace. Agreed with everything he said and did, responded to his *Give us a fag, slag;* turned a blind eye to the nights he didn't come home. (After her mum threw her out Drake had had the grace to find her a flat even though he insisted he didn't live there.) She knew he loved her, his first jail sentence had come on her behalf after he'd thrown the man from the Housing Benefit down the flight of stairs.

It was Caris who was with Jamie that night he choked to death on a fishbone. They'd gone for an Indian after she and Drake had had a row over some girl in the pub and Jamie had taken her to cheer her up. For the life of her she didn't know why Jamie went for fucking fish. He always had chicken tikka. One minute he was cracking her up with some joke and the next he was coughing and clutching at his throat and going blue in the face. When she realised that he wasn't mucking about it was all panic stations, glasses of water from the flustered waiters, then the telephone call for the ambulance after Jamie's eyes rolled backwards and his head flopped forwards. And right to the end his prophecy about the Government came through: for only recently they'd shut down the A&E at Margate and the ambulance had had to scream all the way to Canterbury by which time Jamie was dead.

Drake and Errol went mental after that. Started hanging about with blokes from London and Brighton eager to find markets for the little innocuous envelopes that changed hands underneath the pub tables. Drake grew a beard and went about with a Trinidadian called Clyde whose right to be in the pubs and clubs and eventually on the housing estate he defended with his mouth and fists, and from whom he was initiated to the Calypso records of Mighty Spoiler, Sparrow, and Prince Buster. They ska-ed their way to Ramsgate's hot nightclub Nero's and Club Caprice in Margate, doing business to the blind eyes of the bouncers whilst rocking to *No Woman, No Cry*. Trainers and jeans from Ramsgate market became trainers and jeans from Burton's.

Caris had another baby, and on one of Drake's releases from Sheppey they got married at Ramsgate Registry Office followed by a buffet at the Standard.

After fighting off the attentions of girls called Tracy and Dawn, Errol had fallen for an Irish girl called Siobhan, a nurse at Ramsgate hospital he'd met one lunchtime in the Artillery Arms in between wallpapering a flat for a mate. Siobhan tried to lure him to the idea of the straight and narrow, but all he could get was a job at Tilmanstone Colliery (which, to be fair, he stuck for a week) but he got the shakes even thinking about it – *that fucking lift man, drops like a fucking stone pits of hell man* – and went back to the gratuitous and temporary nature of the work he most enjoyed. All in all, it was meant, he said, eye on the telly with the news of impending closures and miners meaner than him pointing their fingers at the TV cameras and spitting.

When Drake's coughing became noticeable, when he allowed himself to be dragged to the doctors by Caris whose resolute nature had evolved to a nervous laugh after years of being slapped about and shouted down, and on one occasion dragged by the hair down Ramsgate High Street, they were all in for a shock. Drake had cancer of the throat. The years of smoking did not go without comment. The thin warning line on the fag packet suddenly had some relevance. Nobody wanted to elaborate on other experimental ways of getting high, super large reefers, milk bottles, an authentic Moroccan pipe. Grass was the killer, they nodded to themselves, home-grown the worse, always burning the back of your throat.

Hope filled their spirits for a while. Drake went for the operation and even when they took his voice box out it didn't get him down, didn't stop him going down the pub for a pint which he poured down the tube in his throat; though more and more he went with Caris.

When he died it was like the tide had gone out and wasn't coming back. His bar stool stood vacant. Punters went about shaking their heads *you heard about Drake man?* The guy had been larger than life, nothing had fazed him, head to head with coppers the lot. If that could happen to him, it could happen to anyone; life was truly shit man. At least the glass-topped hearse gave him the dignity he deserved.

Siobhan goes to see Errol every day now. She takes the train to Canterbury from Ramsgate, gets a bus to the hospital, sits with him. She never knows what to take him. Grapes were out, as were drinks. He hasn't eaten or drunk for a year now, the tube in his stomach carries everything he needs. Christmas had been the worst, he wouldn't let her refuse his kids a proper dinner, never mind he couldn't eat it. He'd been let out the hospital then, even gone down to the pub where someone was quick to report he'd been seen pouring Scotch down his feeding tube just like his bruv had.

What narked everyone was the unfairness of it all. Those beautiful wild boys who'd roused the bar with Springsteen's *The River*, whose raw coarse voices barked at life, whose pontificating about the world in pubs which had changed with posh furniture and food and banning smoking, of all things... Bastard Life had got them all three in the end, in the same way, in the throat.

Maggie Harris

Unexplored Territory

When Martin Selbington, resident of seventeen Couldson Street, felt angry he shouted at his wife. 'Tart. Slut. Slag.' His wife lived in his head and wasn't a flesh and blood one like the one who lived at number seven; the one who kissed her husband on the lips every morning at eight forty-five, except at weekends when presumably something else happened, though Martin had no idea what.

Martin couldn't say what it was that made him angry. He thought it had something to do with the air. Shouting settled him. He didn't like to think about what he might do if he couldn't settle himself; if the air was stifling. That, like weekends at number seven, was unexplored territory.

Johnny McPherson lived opposite on the even number side. In his thirty-five years he'd lived in all manner of places: lodgings, tower blocks, hostels, squats, bedsits, cockroach-infested flats. And whenever he'd had the misfortune to be housed in an odd number something dreadful had occurred. Now, following the death of his father, he lived alone at number six.

He went into the garden shed and put on his father's brown protective jacket, the one his father had not worn when it was most needed – not that it would have been much use but would have ended up ripped and bloodied like his father who'd been working at an odd number when the accident occurred. He unfolded the deckchair. A cloud of dust blew up into his face. For a moment he was unable to breathe.

Mr Blackshaw lived at number eleven, two doors down from number seven and the unwedded newlyweds. Mr Blackshaw made a point of befriending 'husband' David. He lent him tools, gave him a hand when he said he needed to get to grips with the garden and it was during these moments of male bonding – a concept new to Mr Blackshaw – that David mentioned the couple's non-marital status.

'I want us to be sure first,' he said.

And Mr Blackshaw could see that when Caroline, David's delicate and beautiful 'wife', put an arm around David's waist and stretched up to kiss his cheek that she was only doing what any new wife was supposed to do, because what could she possibly see in a man who spent his lunch hours on treadmills and rowing machines? Mr Blackshaw knew all about these 'open marriages'.

An afternoon in the garden of number seven was rewarded by Caroline emerging from the house to serve tea and toasted teacakes, which Mr Blackshaw said were his favourite. Afterwards Mr Blackshaw would go back to number eleven and take advantage of Mrs Blackshaw – reluctant though she was to leave her sewing – because he needed to get Caroline out of his system.

One Tuesday morning Mrs Blackshaw packed her bags and went to live with her sister. Her leaving came as no surprise to Mr Blackshaw. He knew she'd wanted to go for some time but had been too afraid of the consequences; his infatuation with Caroline provided her with a golden opportunity and she grabbed it. Mr Blackshaw was unfazed. He was perfectly capable of relieving himself without the convenience of the opposite sex, a temporary situation he intended to change.

Martin had finished painting the fronts except for one tiny space that was begging him: 'get me right'. It's common knowledge that a space between two heads is uncharted water; there's a danger of being trapped, either physically, or verbally.

Caroline floated in and out of Mr Blackshaw's life twenty-four-seven. She was in his bed. She was at his breakfast table. She was the star in his collection of explicit videos that he'd kept hidden from Mrs Blackshaw in a suitcase in the spare bedroom.

Once he'd left *Manacled* in the machine and Mrs Blackshaw had pressed the play button expecting to see *The African Queen*. He'd had to slap her hard several times because that was the only way to deal with histrionics. Now he moved his collection to the front room next to the *Encyclopaedia Britannica* – well, not all of it, just the parts he'd found in the cellar when they moved in ten years ago.

He watched Caroline from the back bedroom window. She liked to sunbathe. She wore a tiny sundress with a rich pattern of daisies all over it. He thought of Martin Selbington who was probably also watching because that's what weird people with staring eyes did. Mr Blackshaw looked in the mirror to check that his own eyes weren't of the staring variety.

To catch the kiss required careful planning. Monday he was early and missed it. Tuesday he saw it happen but was too far away. Wednesday's timing was spot on and, when the two faces came together and then parted, the shape he was looking for was formed. The number seven man saw him, looked about to speak, but Martin was gone before words could emerge; Martin was a fast walker with little interest in speech, though he knew enough to get by.

'Good morning, Mrs Bishop.'

'Good morning, Martin.'

After the kiss he started on the backs. They had so much going for them: wooden fences, brick walls, garden furniture – ornate and plain – ponds, trampolines, garages, sheds, hedges, plants in pots, plants in troughs, plants in hanging baskets. Martin hugged himself. He had no one else to hug him. His father had disappeared leaving a note saying that the house was Martin's and that Martin would never see him again. The police thought 'missing person'. Martin thought 'dead', and anyway his father had never once given Martin a hug or even a friendly pat on the back. But he had given him a house.

Johnny McPherson was sitting in his front garden on his cleaned-up deckchair enjoying the sunshine. He liked to observe people as long as he couldn't hear the noises they made. And, although he enjoyed watching the odd numbers, he would never ever walk on their side.

A crow started calling from the top of a tree. It was a sound that warned of imminent danger. He'd heard it the day before his father met his end with a chainsaw. Caw. Caw. It sent shivers down his spine and then out of the blue someone started tinkering with a car engine, revving it up, roaring it like a mad beast and Martin Selbington shouted from across the road, 'Good morning, Mr McPherson', and a neighbour cranked his ancient petrol-fuelled lawn mower at the same time as an irritating whistle established itself on the scene like a timer gone wrong. Johnny, ultra-sensitive to such a cacophony of noise, took to his bed where he covered his head with a black and white striped beach towel that had never seen sand but only Johnny's greasy hair, greasy because Johnny McPherson didn't believe in shampoos instead using margarine as a cleaning product; a method he'd heard described on the top deck of a late night London bus.

It took Martin thirty-one days to complete the ten gardens that stretched in a line between Marshall Crescent and Potters Lane. All done he trimmed each picture, caught the bus into town and went to the shop that sold art materials. He chose an A4 drawing book and some glue and then changed his mind and approached the shop owner Mr Jackson, who must know him by now. 'I've some paintings of my street I don't know what to do with.'

'If you stick them in a book you can't show them to more than one person at a time. If you want to show them that is. Not everyone likes to show off what they do.' Mr Jackson paused. 'Do you?' he said, 'Do you want to show off?'

Martin hadn't thought of showing. It was something he'd have to consider.

Johnny, feeling refreshed, returned to his deckchair to watch the goings-on at numbers seven, eleven and seventeen. Three odd numbers at any one time were enough for him to cope with. He thought about what he was seeing. And he kept on thinking about it: the kissing on the lips, the borrowing of garden tools, the bussing to and from town; he thought about it all so much that the replay button in his head jammed and the residents of seven, eleven and seventeen were trapped in a flurry of never-ending repetitive activity.

Meanwhile, Martin had reasoned that if he did show his pictures, his neighbours would know him better and wouldn't feel the need to speak to him – not that they did but always looked as though they might.

'Bring one in and I'll demonstrate how to make a mount,' Mr Jackson said.

The following week, Martin's exhibition of paintings went up in the library and people who'd never spoken to him asked if it was really him who'd done the pictures and when he said 'yes' they said things like 'very artistic' and 'where did you get the idea from?'. Martin hated questions and comments and shouted at his wife. 'Tart. Slut. Slag.' Words he'd learnt from someone. And when he stopped shouting he heard a knock at the door, the one in his head.

'What?'

'Don't you recognise me? I'm your father, Martin.'

And he remembered where those words came from.

Johnny thought the shouting was probably more to do with the oddness of the house number than anything else. He was down to his last ounce of margarine and, although he ranked 'Tart. Slut. Slag,' as irritating in the extreme, this was a time for shopping, not sleeping. As he closed his gate the crow called loudly and was still calling when he turned out of Couldson Street. He hoped that whatever was going to happen would have nothing to do with him; in the past he'd been a bad boy, but not now.

When Mr Blackshaw saw the exhibition his hackles rose, though no one else seemed offended by the fact that some pervert had been ogling at them and their property. He wondered what Caroline would think of the picture of her and David kissing at the front gate. He went to collect his spade. 'Weren't you just a bit concerned?'

'Not at all,' she said. 'He paints what he sees between and around people and not the people themselves, now that's very clever.'

'But he's been watching you.'

'No harm in that.'

'There's no knowing with people like him. A dark horse.'

'Mrs Bishop says she's known him all her life.'

'Oh well, if Mrs Bishop says,' and he brushed past her to pick up the spade by the back door and he thought he felt her quiver like an excited little poodle begging to be stroked.

'Thank you for the loan,' she said.

'Any time, any time at all.'

'David's going to buy a spade. He said it's not right to be always borrowing things.'

'It's all right with me.'

'Well ... anyway ... that's what he's doing.'

'I'll be off then.' His breathing had become over-amplified, as though he'd just run a hundred metres at full pelt.

At home, gasping for breath, he selected a video. No 'select' was the wrong word. He didn't have time to select. He picked one at random, slotted it into the machine and unfastened his trousers. He was sweating.

Johnny, comforted by his recent purchase, studied the exhibition in the library. Who'd have thought that number seventeen could be so talented? Could it be that odd numbers weren't so bad after all? He wondered about that. No. They had to be as odd as their house numbers. Talent meant nothing. Crazy people had talent. Thank God he lived opposite and not alongside like he had in the past, what a disaster that had been.

When Martin collected his pictures from the library, the librarian asked him to do some more. 'They were very popular,' she said.

Another exhibition! Cats? Birds? The kiss moved, but it didn't take flight. Dead, that's what he needed. Dead cats and birds. Or plants and flowers? But he'd done those. The insides of houses then. He knew where people hid their keys. He knew when they went out. And then he found a dead cat by the side of the road and carried it home in a plastic bag with 'fresh produce' written on the side.

'What's wrong with that Martin bloke?', Mr Blackshaw asked Mrs Bishop.

'I don't know what you mean,' she said. 'Wrong?'

'Well ... you know...'

'Nothing. Nothing's *wrong* with him. Nothing at all. He's no different to anyone else. I don't know why you think he is. He's a private person. We all have things we like to keep to ourselves,' and Mrs Bishop tucked her dress under the leg elastic of her knickers in order to prevent anyone seeing what they shouldn't if the wind happened to blow, and carried on weeding the flower-bed.

Mr Blackshaw went back to his house, his thoughts fixed on Saturday when David at number seven was going away for three days and nights. 'Business,' David had said. 'You can't ignore that,' Mr Blackshaw said. He'd been on 'business' trips himself; he knew the score. 'And don't you worry about Caroline. I'll pop in; make sure she's all right.'

The crow issued a warning salvo of ear-splitting proportions and Johnny McPherson, tucked up in his room at the back of the house, his freshly margarined hair sliding comfortably on the pillow, stuffed the corners of the black and white beach towel into his ears and thanked God that he was an even number.

Across the street at number eleven Mr Blackshaw closed the curtains, slipped in another video and watched the scantily clad Caroline flicker into life. He pulled her towards him. Her breasts pushed against his chest as, with his free hand, he reached behind him for the cuffs. His breathing was laboured, his hands clammy, his mouth dry. Tomorrow was Friday.

And at number seventeen Martin Selbington threw the dead cat in the bin; the creature had started to smell. He put the lid on tight. The bins wouldn't be emptied until Wednesday. But the bad smell was everywhere. Threatening. Stifling.

Maggie Drury

Cold Salt Water

He comes in with his shirt splattered with blood, and I say, 'Honest to God, Kieran.'

'Don't fuss, Mum,' he says, like it's nothing to walk in the house with your nose spread across your face.

'What in Jesus' name happened?' No answer. 'Who were you with?'

'John and Chris.'

'And are they hurt too?'

'Leave it, Mum.'

I put my hand up to his face, but he dips from it. 'It's a rough old place, that dancehall. Tiffany's was it?'

'It's a disco, Mum, not a dancehall.'

And then his father's in the doorway, and I say, 'Will you look at the state of Kieran?' But he's three sheets to the wind himself, so I send him off to bed.

Well, I try to whip the shirt off the boy, but he holds it close around him. So I get a bucket ready: cold water with a good dash of salt. 'Come on now, Kieran,' I say, 'Let's have that shirt.' It's one of his good ones, a Ben Sherman.

He unbuttons it. There are bruises like footprints on his chest.

'Did you get a look at them? Could you describe them to the police?'

'Please, Mum. It doesn't matter.'

'You've bruises all over!'

He flinches as I touch him. I can see that he's trying to hold on to the tears. I know the wobble in that lip, like when his father used to tell him that boys don't cry, so he'd sniff the snot back up into his nose, and pretend he was all right. But a mother knows. But a mother only knows by rummaging in his chest of drawers when he's out, through the piles of pennies and silver in the top drawer from his turned out pockets. I go in there when I'm short of money for the milkman, or need a 50p when the electric's gone. He doesn't like the rattle of the coins in his pockets, and how they spoil the line of his trousers. So they pyramid higher in the drawer, silver on copper, and slip like the coal in the bunker as the drawer opens, heavier each time I pull it out. And that's where I found that thing once, from a packet of three as they call it, and only the one left. I told him what Fr Westland would say. He just laughed. Though there have been times when I've thought, wouldn't we have been glad of one?

He's been worse since he's been working, acting like he's man of the house. Home at six, he slams the back door open against the kitchen dresser – there's a hole in the hardboard now – then he shouts, 'Where's my dinner?' When he was small, I could slap him across the back of the legs, but now he stands above me. I need to stand on a chair to look him in the eye.

'I'm off to bed,' Kieran says. I watch as he climbs the stairs, every step an effort. Whether he sleeps or not, I don't know, but I lie awake next to his snoring father. Every time I close my eyes, I can't stop seeing the footprints on my boy's chest.

In the morning, he's so stiff he can hardly raise an arm, so I knock at Mick Bennett's house, and ask would he tell them at the factory that Kieran won't be in. Then I run Kieran a hot bath to see would it ease him a little, and make him egg and bacon when he's out and dressed. Although it hurts to see him like that, it's nice, in a way, to have my boy to myself, with Jack and the children off for the day.

I've the radio on in the kitchen, and the news headlines come over, of the latest from the IRA, a pub in Guildford, not ten miles up the road. I know there'll be hard stares when I ask for the veg at the greengrocer, when I open my mouth to speak, as if it was me that laid that bomb. 'Are you ready to tell me?' I say, as he wipes the yolk of his egg off the plate with a half-bitten slice of fried bread. He holds up his mug, and I pour some more tea. 'Shall we go to the police?' He half-drains the mug, then slams it down on the table. The tea splashes up the sides then settles again. 'Or was it you that started it? I know your temper.'

The full story of the bombing comes on the radio. 'Switch it off,' he says.

'God knows why your father stands up for that lot,' I say, 'it doesn't do us any good, those of us that have to live here.' He stares at his plate, his fingertips pressing into the edge of the table. 'Is that what the fight was over?' I say.

'It's nothing to do with me, what the Irish get up to,' he says, 'I ain't Irish.'

I wipe my hands on a tea towel and turn to him. 'Only every ounce of blood that flows through your veins.'

'It don't make me Irish.' He butters a slice of bread. I can see how it's bothering him to eat, with his top lip split. Part of me wants to slap him, and the rest of me wants to cradle him. I picture him lying on the ground as the heavy boots hit his chest. And I think of how he's stopped going to The Tara Club, how it's Tiffany's on a Saturday night, out with his packet of three: Durex, approved to British standards.

I go to the bucket where I'd steeped the shirt the night before. The water is pink, the blood seeping into the crystals. I drain the bucket into the sink, rinse the shirt, then run more cold water into the bucket, emptying the remainder of the packet of Saxo into it. I watch the shirt sink, pushing it down so it's covered.

Maria C. McCarthy

Aftermath

She was leaning on the parapet of Magdalen Bridge, looking down at the river, both hands deep in the pockets of a greatcoat too big for her. He had been walking in the Botanic Gardens, for want of anything better to do on a Saturday morning, but there are only so many hours you can kill in a garden in winter. A woman wearing trousers was – slightly – more interesting.

'I heard the war had changed women's habits, but I didn't know it went as far as trousers.' He reached out and fingered the stone, crumbly with lichen.

'And did it change your manners,' she retorted, 'or are you always impertinent to strangers?'

'I beg your pardon. I don't suppose it did me any good, no. But if that's your brother's greatcoat, you look charming in it.'

'It was my cousin's. And I've cut lunch with a tutor to go to his funeral, if you must know.' She seemed to shrink inside the coat. 'This *bloody* influenza.'

There was nothing he could think of to say: he tilted his

head slightly, trying to see her face beyond the curve of dark hair. 'I'm sorry. Very sorry.'

'It only takes the strongest. The best. *It's not fair.*' She turned and began to walk away towards the High Street.

'Doesn't it always? Why else would I still be here... don't go,' he said, and was surprised to see her stop and turn back.

'Why not?' she asked.

'You'll be in trouble, to start with. Out unchaperoned.' He took a few steps towards her.

She began to laugh, a low, bitter noise hardly to be heard above the noise of wheels. 'I was in the base hospital at Rouen when they bombed it, I've washed parts of men my maiden aunts hardly dared think of, and I'm supposed to be in danger on the streets of Oxford!'

'I know; ridiculous,' he said. 'I've run messages back of the trenches hoping like hell that the star shells don't show me up, and I have to be back in college by ten past nine.'

'You too?' They stopped and looked at each other, face to face for the first time. 'Béthune,' she said. 'You were after Béthune. And...' she giggled. 'You had *measles!*'

'Yes. My mighty war.' He smiled. 'The perils of being billeted on a family.' He took off his hat. 'I thought it was you, when... when you spoke. The tall nurse who brought in rabbits for the pot. We used to wonder who shot them.'

'I did, as it happens. I'm a good shot. Some of us were brought up in the country.' She brushed her hair out of her eyes in a gesture he had last seen when she was down on her knees scrubbing the floor by Captain Carrow's bed.

'Despite the maiden aunts,' he said.

'*By* the maiden aunts. I used to escape when I could.' She looked at him, laughter glinting in her eyes. 'Am I going to be in worse trouble if I go back alone, or if you come with me?'

He held out his hat. 'Put that on. It should pass muster as far as... ?'

'The Woodstock Road, or until someone notices my heels. Thank you.' She crammed it on to her head, and tucked the ends of her hair up under it.

'Don't tell me you're a Home Student.'

'Do I look like one?' She looked at him again. She *was* tall; her eyes were almost at a level with his.

'No. You don't.' He adjusted the hat to the correct angle. 'That's better.'

'Then the honour of my college is safe, at least.'

They crossed Longwall, and walked for a while in silence: past the Mitre, with the cold wind at their backs, and past the University Church. Suddenly he said, 'It doesn't seem real, you know. Being back. I used to hold on to this place, in my head, when it was all mud and noise out there. Now... ' They crossed Turl Street and turned right, changing places so that he was on the outside of the pavement still.

'Now,' she said, '*it's* real enough. But we don't belong. We're like ghosts here, but still living. The first years – they seem so shrill and silly. I can hardly bear it, sometimes.' She glanced sideways into the window of a jeweller's shop.

'Young and innocent. Don't blame them. You've earned the right to be here, if anyone has.' He shivered. 'Could we move on?'

'I'm sorry. You must be cold without your hat.' She moved as if to take his left arm, but remembered herself when he stepped forward.

'No. I dreamt about this street last night. That the paving stones were all thrown up, as if by shells, and underneath was – like No Man's Land. All bones and bits and – '. Though the wall was to his left, he leaned on it briefly with his right arm. 'I'm sorry. I should stop.'

'It sounds as if you've earned your place here too,' she said.

'What about the ones who didn't make it? Didn't they

earn theirs?' He stood straight again, and walked off not waiting for her.

'Yes they did,' she said fiercely, half-running to catch up. 'Of *course* they did. And some thought they had it, like Jim, and then the influenza got them all the same. Is that fair?'

'Fair? No. The way of the world? Probably.' After a few minutes he asked, 'Do you remember them all? Jack LeStrange from the House, and the Canadians? That boy from the Naval Brigade, and Ned Carrow who got in such a rage when someone stole his precious souvenir Mauser?'

'I remember them,' she said. 'We all teased Captain Carrow dreadfully, when it turned out the rifle wasn't missing after all.'

'Wasn't it? I don't remember that.'

She stopped in her tracks suddenly, as if startled, though it might have been to avoid the cyclist turning, un-signalling and un-belled, out of Broad Street. 'No – you wouldn't. It was after... '

'Oh, yes. Of course.' His voice, which had been so animated, deadened suddenly. 'You know, my mamma always used to tell me, be careful what you ask for. You might get it.'

Broad Street was behind them, the blank corner of Balliol to their right as they turned northward into St Giles. She said, gently, tentatively, 'I remember what you asked for.'

He laughed, tipping his head back and running his hand through the short, fair hair. 'I was desperate, wasn't I? I'm such a coward. Just a nice little Blighty one, enough to send me home discharged unfit for service.'

A few of last year's leaves still hung withered on the plane trees, or cracked under their feet. He kicked at them.

She bit her lip. 'You were running a high fever. You might not have meant it.'

'Oh, I meant it all right. And I got it, didn't I? Thanks

to some German sniper and *his* fancy Mauser. I tell you, our boys really used to envy them that optical sight.' He shrugged. 'I suppose it was damn silly of me to go sight-seeing so near the lines.'

She said, in a strained voice, 'Probably. I think Matron was more upset by the fact that you disobeyed orders.'

'I dare say. She was a tartar. If she ever heard that my left hand's totally useless, she probably regards it as a judgement.' They walked on in silence until he said, 'We're almost up to the church. You'd better cross the road.'

'I had, hadn't I? The path by the south door is best.' They dropped into single file between the low walls, and crossed the Woodstock Road.

'Thank you for seeing me back,' she said. 'I must have taken you out of your way.'

'Not necessarily. Maybe I'll go for a walk,' he said lightly. 'Out to Port Meadow to read Housman, or something pathetically romantic like that.'

'Not much like Shropshire, is it?' she said. 'I'm from Church Stretton.' They passed the line of shops, and St Aloysius' Church, primly drawn back from the road.

He stopped by the corner of the college, against the railings, and said, 'He *knows*, though, doesn't he? Old Housman? *That is the land of lost content.* Or if he doesn't know, how come he says it for me?'

She finished the quotation for him. '*Those happy highways where I went/And cannot come again.* But you are here again, after all.'

'Happy? Maybe.' He shook his head. 'Don't mind me. I'm... glad we met.' He looked sideways at her. 'So Ned Carrow's Mauser turned up after all?'

'Yes. A few days later. Where it was all along, hidden up in his bedsprings.' She handed his hat back to him and shook her hair loose. 'Thanks for the loan. I'll try to get in with someone else, or go round to Walton Street and climb through Cicely's window.'

'Take care,' he said. 'What's for dinner in hall tonight? Rabbit?'

Her laughter was unconvincing. 'If it is, I shan't eat it. Never again.'

He said, slowly, 'Do you still shoot?'

'Not any more.' She looked at him, a crease between her brows. 'Why do you ask?'

'No reason in the world.' He watched her for a moment, and then said, 'I could have wished the sniper had gone for the other hand. I'd been looking for a decent excuse to give my mamma for not using the right one, ever since I started school.' He stepped back as a cluster of students arrived and crowded round the wicket door. 'Here's your Trojan Horse.'

She didn't lift her feet high enough, and stumbled at the threshold. 'You're left-handed?' she said.

'I was. That sniper did something my mamma never could.' He touched his hat to her. 'I won't shake hands, if you don't mind.' And he went on, northward, left hand in his pocket. For a while she watched him, and then began to cry silently, clinging to the edge of the door. Under her hands it was as smooth and worn as a rifle stock.

Jane Stemp

Biographies of the authors

Jenny Cross taught creative writing and ran a reading group in Canterbury. She once owned a shop called Ritzy Bitz, danced on Top of the Pops, cut wire at Greenham Common and has dirty fingernails as she is mostly in the garden. She enjoys cooking for friends, walking the dog with her husband David, and is Chair of The Friends of Herne Bay Museum. Jenny graduated from the University of Kent with a degree in English Literature and Comparative Literature two days before her fiftieth birthday.

Maggie Drury writes plays, novels, short stories and occasionally poetry. Her play *Not Knowing Who We Are* was performed at The Blue Elephant Theatre in 2007. *Enjoy* was performed at the Lounge on the Farm Festival and at The Horsebridge Centre Whitstable in 2012.

June English was born in Dover, Kent, in 1936. As a mature student, she read English and History at the University of Kent, followed by an MA in Humanities. Her first collection of poetry, *Counting the Spots* (Acumen 2000), was short-listed for the BBC New Voices programme. Two further collections *The Sorcerer's Arc* (2004) and *Sunflower Equations* (2008) were published by Hearing Eye. She has also published a chapter in *Writing Your Self: Transforming Personal Material*, edited by John Killick and Myra Schneider (Continuum 2009). She is presently Poet in Residence for Sing for your Life.

Maggie Harris has published five collections of poetry; her first, *Limbolands,* won the Guyana Prize for Literature 2000. Her memoir of growing up in Guyana, *Kiskadee Girl,* was published by Kingston University Press in 2011. She has also recorded a CD of poems for children, *Anansi Meets Miss Muffet*. Her collection of short stories, *Canterbury Tales on a Cockcrow Morning* (awarded a New Writing South Bursary), is published by Cultured Llama (2012). A writer and an artist, she has been International Teaching Fellow at Southampton University, a literature festival organiser and runs workshops for both children and adults. Her exhibition, *From Broadstairs with Love,* ran at The Old Lookout Gallery, Broadstairs, in June 2012.

Mark Holihan, a writer and artist, is a former Californian now transplanted to Kent. He has been published in various anthologies and magazines, is a winner of the Phelan award and was recently shortlisted for the Bridport prize.

Sarah Jenkin started writing in 2004 at an adult education class. She swore then that she would write anything but poetry. Since then she has written mostly poetry and has now branched out into writing plays. She was chair of the Medway Mermaids writing group, and is an occasional contributor to the ME4 writing collective. Sarah's work has been published in several anthologies, including *The Mermaid,* the *Medway Festival Fringe, All Sorts* and in publications including *Touchstone, Encyclopaedia Citaecephale* and *Blithe Spirit,* the journal for the British Haiku Society. Her mini-plays, *At the Beginning* and *Bad Signal,* were recently performed by 17percent.

Philip Kane is an award-winning writer, storyteller and artist whose books include *The Wildwood King* (Capall Bann 1997) and *The Hicklebaum Papers* (Mezzanine Press 2010), as well as his latest poetry collection *Unauthorised Person* (Cultured Llama 2012). He is a founding member of the London Surrealist Group. Over the past thirty years he has built up an international reputation, publishing and exhibiting in a number of countries including Spain and the USA. He is currently Artistic Director for the Rochester Literature Festival.

Luigi Marchini was brought up in London where he spent many a happy maths and physics lesson at the National Film Theatre.

Maria C. McCarthy's first poetry collection *strange fruits* is published by Cultured Llama (2011) in association with WordAid, with all profits going to Macmillan Cancer Support. Her story collection *As Long As It Takes* is awaiting discovery by the publishing fairy, who will magically transform her into a writer with the riches of J.K. Rowling.

Rosemary McLeish was born in 1945. She started writing and painting when she was 40, and has had poems published in anthologies and magazines, and shown them in several exhibitions. She has self-published two collections. She lived for 25 years in Glasgow, where she did an MPhil in Creative Writing in 2005. She now lives in Kent with her husband.

Gillian Moyes has had poems published in several magazines and anthologies and is co-author of two books published by Common Room Poets. She enjoys walking in the countryside each day with her dog and has worked as a volunteer for Kent Wildlife Trust on conservation projects. She is a basic skills tutor for Adult Education and has helped some students to read and write for the first time in their lives.

Bethany W. Pope is a UK-based writer originally from the Southern United States. She and her husband currently live in Wiltshire. She earned her Master's Degree in Creative Writing from University of Wales Trinity Saint David and her PhD in Creative Writing from Aberystwyth University. She has worked as a farmhand, a midwife for cattle, a keeper at a children's zoo, a veterinarian's assistant and a restaurant car-hop. Her first poetry collection, *A Radiance,* was released by Cultured Llama in 2012; her second collection *Persephone in the Underworld* is to be published by Rufus Books. There is much more to come.

Hilda Sheehan is a mother of five children and has been a psychiatric nurse and Montessori teacher. She is editor of *Domestic Cherry* magazine and also works for Swindon Artswords (Literature Development) and the Swindon Festival of Poetry.

Fiona Sinclair's work has been published in numerous publications. Her second poetry collection *A Game of Hide and Seek* was published in July 2012 by Indigo Dreams. She is the editor of the online poetry magazine *Message in a Bottle*.

Jane Stemp was born in Lewisham in 1961 and grew up in Surrey. She studied English at Somerville College, Oxford, and librarianship at Aberystwyth. After marrying in 1999, she now lives with Robin and several thousand books in Somerset. Her present job is with the Navy in Hampshire. Jane's novels

Waterbound (1996) and *Secret Songs* (1997) were short-listed for the NASEN Children's Book Award. *Secret Songs,* partly inspired by her own experience of hearing loss, was also short-listed for the Guardian Children's Fiction Prize. When Jane is not writing or working she enjoys cooking historical recipes and singing – not, so far, simultaneously.

Richard Thomas is a poet from Plymouth, UK, with a diploma in Creative Writing, poems published in journals and anthologies internationally and a poem shortlisted for the National Poetry Competition 2011. Richard is the editor of *Symmetry Pebbles,* a poetry e-zine – www.symmetrypebbles.com. His first collection of poems *The Strangest Thankyou,* from which the poems in *Unexplored Territory* were taken, is published by Cultured Llama (2012).

Vicky Wilson is a writer, editor, publisher and educator. She was Poet in Residence at Brent Museum and Archives 2011–2012 and her guidebook *London's Houses* was published by Metro Publications in 2011. She is also a co-founder of WordAid, a Kent collective that publishes poetry to raise money for charity. She is currently exploring how place and music can provide inspiration.

Acknowledgements

Jenny Cross
'Fat Woman', was runner up in a 'Split the Lark' competition, where it was originally titled 'Lament of a Dieting Woman'.

June English
'Higher Nature' and 'Sabbath' appear in her collection *Sunflower Equations* (Hearing Eye 2008).

Maggie Harris
'My Daughters: a Poem for Mothers Day' was published on Facebook on Mother's Day, 2012. 'The Calypsonians of Ramsgate' is published in *Canterbury Tales on a Cockcrow Morning* (Cultured Llama 2012).

Sarah Jenkin
'Medway Mermaid' was previously published as 'A Mermaid's Tail' in the members section of the Hags, Harlots, Heroines website (March 2005).

Philip Kane
'River's Edge' was first published in *Penumbra* issue 2 (Autumn 2007). 'city's little heart' was first published as a pamphlet (of the full sequence) by Mezzanine Press (1994). 'carole in the supermarket' and 'johnnie & carole have a row' were previously anthologised in *The Industry of Letters* (Mezzanine Press/ KCC 1996). 'johnnie & carole have a row' also appeared in *The Medway Scene* (Urban Fox Press 2003) and *The Arts in Medway* (Urban Fox Press 2004).

Maria C. McCarthy
'Cold Salt Water' was published in *The Frogmore Papers*, 75, 2010 and was winner of the Save As Prose Awards, 2009. An earlier version of 'Pioneer' was published in the *Norwich Writers Open Poetry Competition Anthology*, 2012.

Rosemary McLeish
'Charcoal Drawing' won first prize in the Speakeasy Poetry Competition in 2007.

Bethany W. Pope
'Radiance' is published in her collection *A Radiance* (Cultured Llama 2012).

Fiona Sinclair
'When a sex symbol takes to sensible shoes' was published in *Grey Sparrow Journal*, 2011. 'Singing Group' was published in *Pulsar Magazine*, 2012.

Jane Stemp
'Aftermath' was first published in *The Lost College & Other Oxford Stories* (OxPens 2008).

Richard Thomas
'Flamingo', 'Twenty Five' and 'Arise to thy Lyre' appear in his collection *The Strangest Thankyou* (Cultured Llama 2012).

Cultured Llama Publishing

hungry for poetry
thirsty for fiction

Cultured Llama was born in a converted stable. This creature of humble birth drank greedily from the creative source of the poets, writers, artists and musicians that visited, and soon the llama fulfilled the destiny of its given name.

Cultured Llama is a publishing house, a multi-arts events promoter and a fundraiser for charity. It aspires to quality from the first creative thought through to the finished product.

www.culturedllama.co.uk

Also published by Cultured Llama

A Radiance
by Bethany W. Pope

Paperback; 70pp; 203 x 127 mm;
978-0-9568921-3-3; June 2012
Cultured Llama

Family stories and extraordinary images glow throughout this compelling debut collection from an award-winning author, like the disc of uranium buried in her grandfather's backyard. *A Radiance* 'gives glimpses into a world both contemporary and deeply attuned to history – the embattled history of a family, but also of the American South where the author grew up.'

> 'A stunning debut collection… these poems invite us to reinvent loss as a new kind of dwelling, where the infinitesimal becomes as luminous as ever.'
>
> Menna Elfyn

'*A Radiance* weaves the voices of four generations into a rich story of family betrayal and survival, shame and grace, the visceral and sublime. A sense of offbeat wonder at everyday miracles of survival and love both fires these poems and haunts them – in a good way.'

Tiffany S. Atkinson

'An exhilarating and exceptional new voice in poetry.'

Matthew Francis

Also published by Cultured Llama

strange fruits
by Maria C. McCarthy

Paperback; 72pp; 203 x 127 mm;
978-0-9568921-0-2; July 2011
Cultured Llama (in association with
WordAid.org.uk)

Maria is a poet of remarkable skill, whose work offers surprising glimpses into our 21st-century lives – the 'strange fruits' of our civilisation or lack of it. Shot through with meditations on the past and her heritage as 'an Irish girl, an English woman', *strange fruits* includes poems reflecting on her urban life in a Medway town and as a rural resident in Swale.

Maria writes, and occasionally teaches creative writing, in a shed at the end of her garden.

All profits from the sale of *strange fruits* go to Macmillan Cancer Support, Registered Charity Number 261017.

'Maria McCarthy writes of the poetry process: "There is a quickening early in the day" ('Raising Poems'). A quickening is certainly apparent in these humane poems, which are both natural and skilful, and combine the earthiness and mysteriousness of life. I read *strange fruits* with pleasure, surprise and a sense of recognition.'

Moniza Alvi, author of *Europa*

Also published by Cultured Llama

Canterbury Tales on a Cockcrow Morning
by Maggie Harris

Paperback; 136pp; 203x127 mm;
978-0-9568921-6-4; September 2012
Cultured Llama

Maggie Harris brings warmth and humour to her *Canterbury Tales on a Cockcrow Morning*, and tops them with a twist of calypso.

Here are pilgrims old and new: Eliot living in 'This Mother Country' for half a century; Samantha learning that country life is not like in the magazines.

There are stories of regret, longing and wanting to belong; a sense of place and displacement resonates throughout.

> 'Finely tuned to dialogue and shifting registers of speech, Maggie Harris' fast-moving prose is as prismatic as the multi-layered world she evokes. Her Canterbury Tales, sharply observed, are rich with migrant collisions and collusions.'
>
> John Agard

Also published by Cultured Llama

The Strangest Thankyou
by Richard Thomas

Paperback; 98pp; 203x127 mm;
978-0-9568921-5-7; October 2012
Cultured Llama

Richard Thomas's debut poetry collection embraces the magical and the mundane, the exotic and the everyday, the surreal rooted in reality.

Grand poetic themes of love, death and great lives are cut with surprising twists and playful use of language, shape, form and imagery.

The poet seeks 'an array of wonder' in "Dig" and spreads his 'riches' throughout *The Strangest Thankyou*.

> 'He has long been one to watch, and with this strong, diverse collection Richard Thomas is now one to read. And re-read.'
>
> Matt Harvey

Also published by Cultured Llama

Unauthorised Person
by Philip Kane

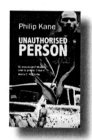

Paperback; 74pp; 203x127 mm;
978-0-9568921-4-0; November 2012
Cultured Llama

Philip Kane describes *Unauthorised Person* as a 'concept album' of individual poems, sequences, and visuals, threaded together by the central motif of the River Medway.

This collection draws together poems written and images collected over 27 years, exploring the psychogeography of the people and urban landscapes of the Medway Towns, where 'chatham high street is paradise enough' ("johnnie writes a quatrain").

> 'This collection shows a poet whose work has grown in stature to become strong, honest and mature. Yet another voice has emerged from the Medway region that I'm sure will be heard beyond our borders. The pieces here vary in tone, often lyrical, sometimes prosaic but all show a deep rooted humanity and a political (with a small p) sensibility.'
>
> Bill Lewis